Cox

Books should be returned or renewed by the last
date above. Renew by phone **03000 41 31 31** or
online *www.kent.gov.uk/libs*

Libraries Registration & Archives

D1491547

C333743384

War and Peace

Adapted by
Mary Sebag-Montefiore

Illustrated by Simona Bursi

Reading consultant: Alison Kelly

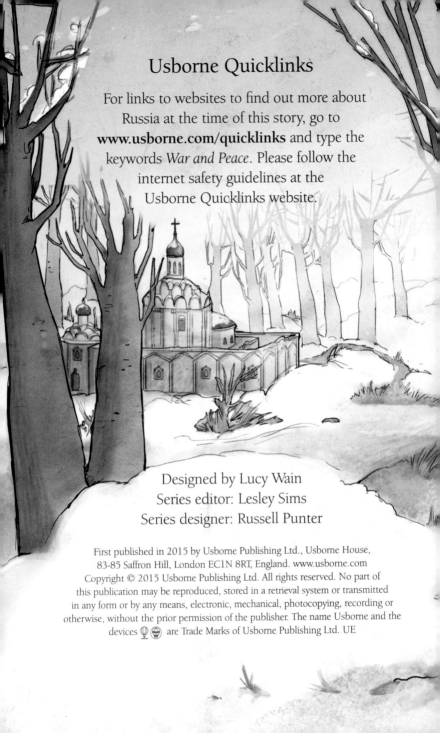

Usborne Quicklinks

For links to websites to find out more about
Russia at the time of this story, go to
www.usborne.com/quicklinks and type the
keywords *War and Peace*. Please follow the
internet safety guidelines at the
Usborne Quicklinks website.

Designed by Lucy Wain
Series editor: Lesley Sims
Series designer: Russell Punter

First published in 2015 by Usborne Publishing Ltd., Usborne House,
83-85 Saffron Hill, London EC1N 8RT, England. www.usborne.com

Contents

Introduction 4
The characters in the story 6

PART ONE: Peace is far away

Chapter 1   Pierre's first party   8
Chapter 2   Money can't buy love   14
Chapter 3   Andrew's first battle   18
Chapter 4   Unanswerable questions   24

PART TWO: Natasha and the end of war

Chapter 5   A breath of hope   29
Chapter 6   Joy and sorrow   32
Chapter 7   The battle of Borodino   42
Chapter 8   The burning of Moscow   50
Chapter 9   A heart of gold   56

Map of Napoleon's invasion of Russia   62
in 1812

Introduction

War and Peace is set in Russia, at the beginning of the 19th century, during the reign of Tsar Alexander I. His family, the Romanovs, had ruled for almost 200 years and Russia was largely made up of an extremely wealthy, land-owning aristocracy and millions of serfs – slaves who were tied to the land.

It was a time of turmoil. Some Russians were starting to question their whole way of life, looking

to western Europe for a new approach, though most wanted to continue as they had for centuries.

At the same time, the self-styled Emperor of France, Napoleon Bonaparte, was determined to conquer and unite all of Europe. He had already led his 'Grande Armée' to victory in most of the west and, in 1812, he invaded Russia. In the terrible war that followed, over 500,000 men died.

This is the story of those fateful few years – of war and peace, despair and courage, and, finally, love and wisdom.

Pierre Bezukhov

Vasili Kuragin

The characters
in the story

Helene Kuragina

Anatole Kuragin

Andrew Bolkonski

Lisa Bolkonskaya

Natasha Rostova

Nicholas Bolkonski

PART ONE

Peace is far away

Chapter 1

Pierre's first party

Pierre Bezukhov looked different from everyone else at the party. All the other guests were princes and princesses, all perfumed, all glittering in jewels, silk and embroidery. Pierre was tall, awkward, rather fat and wore glasses. He was the illegitimate son of a dying duke, and since he was poor, everyone, particularly his elderly cousin, Prince Vasili, considered him to be a rank below themselves. Pierre had only one friend at the party: Prince Andrew Bolkonski.

Pierre listened as his hostess shrieked.

"I HATE Napoleon. His army marches through Europe conquering every country he wants. No one will help. England and Austria are useless. Only Russia can save Europe! Well? What do you think, Vasili?"

"What can one say?" replied Vasili languidly, watching his stumbling son, Anatole, and his lovely daughter, Helene. He'd brought Helene here to find a rich husband – any husband would do who could be persuaded to pay off Anatole's huge debts.

"I... oh... introduce me," whispered Pierre to Andrew, unable to take his eyes off Helene. Her beauty was cold but alluring. She was compelling.

Andrew shrugged. He was watching his wife, Lisa, as she danced, his lips curled in a sneer. "Don't ever marry, Pierre," he said. "You lose your freedom. I'm chained to parties and gossip and silly women who think of nothing..."

Pierre was astonished. He'd always thought fate had smiled on Andrew – handsome, rich, well-connected and good at everything – the opposite, in fact, of himself. Andrew's life shone with success, and on top of that, Lisa was expecting a baby.

Lisa must have sensed Andrew's despising

glance. She ran to him crying, "I wish you weren't going away to fight! I'll be lonely without you, waiting for the baby to arrive."

"You're joining the army! Why?" asked Pierre as Lisa, receiving no answer from Andrew, turned away in despair.

"Because I hate my life," Andrew replied. "Besides, if men did not fight for other men's beliefs, there would be no wars."

"No war – how splendid! Are you even right to be fighting Napoleon? He believes in free speech, the freedom of the press and equality."

Pierre's loud voice stopped the buzz of conversation in a sudden, appalled silence. Everyone hated and feared Napoleon.

"I don't want that buffoon near Helene," thought Vasili, beckoning his daughter over.

Pierre watched her moving lightly through the throng, smiling as if graciously allowing everyone the privilege of admiring her loveliness.

"You like Helene?" Anatole mumbled to Pierre, slurring his words. "You'll never get her. Come along later this evening to my party. Much better than this."

At Anatole's door late that night, the stench of sweat and smoke billowed into the street. Pierre heard screams of laughter and a bear growling. Inside, the men – it was a party only for men – were pulling the bear's chain to irritate it. Pierre, soon as caught up in the madness as the rest, lifted the bear and danced around the room with it.

He never remembered the rest of the evening – how they pushed the bear into a carriage on the way to see some actresses, how a policeman tried to interfere, how they tied the bear to the policeman and threw them both in the river.

Pierre thought a little of Andrew. Andrew would never go to such a party or behave like that, but there was something in Pierre's character that loved recklessness.

Chapter 2
Money can't buy love

Old Prince Vasili knew his cousin, Pierre's father, was dying, and visited him, not to say goodbye, but to discover the rich old man's heir. He hoped for a legacy himself. Secretly he searched for the will, but when he found it, he was horrified. The heir was Pierre. He also found legal documents revoking Pierre's illegitimacy.

Pierre would become Count Bezukhov, owner of estates, mansions, serfs and the biggest fortune in Russia.

I should get it, Vasili thought, *not that buffoon*.

He was just about to destroy the will, hands poised to burn it in the fire, when another cousin attending the deathbed interrupted him. He was supporting Pierre, who was grief-stricken.

"All is over," wept Pierre. He'd loved his father.

Putting on a solemn, sympathetic expression, Vasili spoke in a deep, cooing voice, "My condolences, dear boy. But congratulations on your inheritance. Let me help you accustom yourself to your new fortune."

Instantly, he decided: *Helene shall marry Pierre.* He would invite Pierre to stay; having him close to her would surely do the trick.

Pierre quickly fell under the spell of Helene's beauty. He was in some confusion. When he had been poor, everyone ignored him. Now he was rich, he was universally considered witty, wise and brilliant. He felt a bright future dangling ahead of him, glimpsed but not yet attained. When he was with Helene, this feeling crystallized into longing for her. She would hover so close to him that he breathed her scent and felt the warmth of her body, despite the cold look in her eyes.

I must marry her, he thought. *I know something is not right, but I can't help myself.*

Six weeks later, they were married and living in Pierre's new, large and richly-furnished house in St. Petersburg. Vasili, delighted, persuaded Pierre to settle a generous allowance on himself and his son.

A lucky man, the world thought Pierre, to have such a beautiful, charming wife.

Once, Pierre asked Helene if she'd like to have

children. She laughed contemptuously, her eyes as blank and hard as a reptile's.

"Do you really think I'd want children with *you*? I have your money. Get out! You bore me."

So this is what I've married, Pierre agonized. *I knew when I told her 'I love you' that it was a mistake, and now I'm stuck with her.*

Chapter 3
Andrew's first battle

Since joining the army, Prince Andrew had changed. No longer frustrated, trapped by endless dull parties, he felt happy at last – busy, fit and active. Now he was off to Austerlitz, in the Austrian Empire, where the enemy French troops were advancing. He loved the journey, headed by drummers drumming, soldiers singing, horses clattering and spurs jingling.

He knew, though, that Napoleon had beaten the Austrians, Russia's allies, at Ulm. That meant the campaign was half lost already. Everyone felt it unlikely that the Russians could defeat the invincible French.

We're like a clock, Andrew thought, *wound up, the wheels setting in motion an aim far beyond each individual mechanism. Our battle is just one movement on the dial of human history, though it's life or death to each soldier.*

He dedicated himself to give all he had to Russia.

On the eve of battle, the air was dense with fog. Austrian allies galloped to the Russian army's left flank; the central section of Russian soldiers separated from the right flank, and was ordered to join them. That meant the cavalry had to pass in front of the infantry, an unheard-of move. For a while, confusion swirled like the fog.

It didn't really matter, everyone thought, because there was plenty of time to get into position. Napoleon was at least six miles away.

But Napoleon, the great strategist, had seized

his chance. The Russians thought they knew where he was? Well, he'd surprise them.

Under cover of the night and blanket of mist, his troops crept close. At daybreak, as the sun emerged, he signed for the firing to begin.

Andrew was the first to see a column of French soldiers. *The moment has come*, he told himself, as gunshot, smoke and fleeing soldiers formed a triptych of terror. Even the standard bearer ran, dropping the Russian flag, to be trampled and torn by the footsteps of frightened men.

"NO!" Andrew yelled, choked with anger.

He leaped from his horse and grabbed the flag,
calling to the soldiers: "FORWARD!"

Holding it upright, despite its heavy weight,
he charged on, to lead the battalion to face
the enemy.

He heard the whistle of bullets all around, and
screams of agony as soldiers fell to the ground.
He felt impelled to carry on, even when a bullet
shot through his side. Then he grew angrier
because the pain distracted him.

What's this?... I'm falling... he thought, seconds before he collapsed.

Above him, he saw the sky, immeasurably high, quiet and peaceful, utterly different from the shouting and fighting a moment before.

Why didn't I realize before? he wondered. *How happy I am to have found out now. All is vanity and lies, save that infinite sky.*

In the evening, Napoleon surveyed his victory, walking among the fallen Russian soldiers.

"A fine death," he remarked, gazing at Andrew.

Andrew was aware that it was Napoleon who spoke, but he wished only for help to bring him back to life, which seemed so beautiful now he had learned today to understand it. He collected all his strength and groaned.

"Ah. He's alive. Put him on a stretcher and bring him to the field hospital."

With every jolt as he was carried, Andrew felt almost unendurable pain. But then he thought of the peace the sky had promised and of Lisa, his pregnant wife, waiting for him at home.

Chapter 4
Unanswerable questions

Weeks later, Princess Lisa received a letter from Andrew's colonel.

Your husband is missing, perhaps dead. He fell as a hero, with the flag in his hands at the head of his regiment. His body has not been found...

She didn't weep; she could think only of her unborn baby.

"I will love you so," she promised it, stroking her growing belly as the months passed.

When the birth pains began, the servants helped her to bed and sent for the doctor.

A clatter of horses' hooves... footsteps running to her door. Lisa glanced from her bed to see – not the doctor, but Andrew, back from the war, his fur coat dusted with snow. He was pale and thin, with a changed, strangely softened expression.

"My darling," he said, a word he'd never used to her before, kissing her. But Lisa hardly realized he'd come. She was in the grip of unbelievable, torturing pains. When the doctor arrived, he threw Andrew out of the room to attend to his patient.

A terrible shriek tore the air, followed by a baby's wail. Just as Andrew realized the joyful meaning of that sound, the doctor beckoned him in. Lisa was lying perfectly still, in the same position he'd found her just five minutes before. She was dead.

Andrew felt something give way in his soul. He felt that he was guilty of a sin he could never forget. Too late to tell her now all the things in his heart. Sobbing, he picked up the child, a baby boy, in his arms. Then he kissed, this time for farewell, the waxen pallor of his wife's face.

Pierre's marriage, meanwhile, was at breaking point. He'd heard gossip that Helene was seeing a man named Dolokhov.

Pierre, miserable and furious, pictured Helene, in love not with him but with Dolokhov. He imagined his friends thinking him a fool, unable

to make his wife happy. His temper raging, he confronted Dolokhov.

"You scoundrel!" he yelled. "I challenge you to a duel!"

"Tomorrow," Dolokhov agreed.

The duel took place in a clearing in a pine forest covered in melting snow. The antagonists stood apart, their swords stuck into the ground to mark the distance.

Pierre had never even held a pistol before. *I want to run away, or bury myself*, he thought.

He fired, shuddering, not expecting so loud a bang. Through the smoke, he saw Dolokhov lying senseless in the snow.

"Folly... folly..." he muttered, horrified, convinced he'd killed Dolokhov. The man was only wounded, but Pierre felt as guilty as a murderer, because he'd hurt Helene's friend.

Helene was waiting for Pierre at home. "You know what this duel proves?" she taunted him. "That you're an idiot. I like Dolokhov because he's cleverer than you, but I'm not in love with him."

"I think we'd better separate," said Pierre, mumbling like a broken man.

"Only if you give me a fortune."

"Have what you want," Pierre said. "I shall leave you and go away somewhere."

Pierre didn't care where he went. He was tortured by his thoughts. *What is bad? What is good?* he wondered. *What is love? What should I live for?* And then, *What unseen Power governs life?* He could only think of one answer to them all: *You'll die and know everything, or cease asking.*

But the thought of death was also dreadful.

PART TWO
Natasha and the end of war

Chapter 5
A breath of hope

For many months Pierre wandered over Russia. He met a group of holy men who helped him. Listening and talking to them, he realized he had always thought about himself, not others. He'd been idle, self-indulgent, quick to anger. He decided to change his whole attitude to life.

First, he freed all his serfs. Then he built hospitals and schools on his estates.

Doing good is easy, he told himself. *How little we pay attention to it.* He resolved to take Helene back; he would try to make things work out.

Before doing so, he visited his old friend, Andrew. Both had suffered, Pierre in his marriage, and Andrew from his wounds at Austerlitz and in the death of his wife.

"I believe God wants us to make ourselves happy trying to do good," Pierre announced shyly, still in awe of Andrew.

They were taking an evening stroll, with Andrew's baby son, Nicholas. Pierre pointed to the sky, filled with the warm yellow glow of sunset.

"Up there, in glorious space, is the Whole we strive for."

Andrew was gazing sadly at his little Nicholas. The sky reminded him of his experience at Austerlitz, and then, for the first time since Lisa's death, something joyful awoke within him.

He wondered if, maybe, a new life awaited him

one day. "You're right. We should believe in the possibility of happiness."

He kissed little Nicholas, feeling grateful to Pierre. He'd refused an invitation to a ball that week. Maybe he should rouse himself from his solitude and accept.

And, at that ball, Andrew met a young girl named Natasha Rostova.

Chapter 6
Joy and sorrow

Natasha had never been to a grand ball before. On the way, sitting in the dark, chilly carriage, she had imagined brightly lit rooms, flowers, music, dances, the Emperor of Russia, and all the brilliant people of St. Petersburg arrayed in grandeur. Her feet tingled inside her dancing shoes. She knew she ought to put on a majestic air, as she'd been taught, but when she arrived and saw everything was even better than she'd pictured it, she couldn't help showing her excitement.

"Beautiful," said her host, kissing her fingers. "A young girl in a white dress, with a rose in her hair – just right for the occasion."

She felt shy, certain the evening was preparing to bring her either misery or bliss.

Her parents pointed out to her all the notables.

"There's the lovely Countess Helene Bezukhov, standing with her husband, Pierre, the stout one in spectacles, beside her. And there's Helene's brother, Anatole."

"Very handsome," Natasha murmured.

"And Prince Andrew Bolkonski, in a white uniform. Ah, he wishes to be introduced to you."

"Will you dance?" Andrew asked.

Natasha danced exquisitely. Her feet were swift and light, her face shone with delight, and Andrew, embracing her slender waist, felt her charm, like wine, warming his heart.

"I want her for my wife," Andrew thought, while Natasha, whirling in his arms to the music, was thinking, "I'm so happy... There can't be evil in the world if I feel like this."

After the ball, Andrew saw Natasha often.

He told Pierre, "When I'm with her, all is joy and light; when we're apart, I feel gloom and darkness."

"I understand," said Pierre sadly, thinking of his own marriage that had brought him nothing but darkness. Natasha's appeal and her readiness to love made him think, *If only I were free, I too could have chosen her.* "Truly, I'm glad for you. Will you propose?"

"I have already, and she's accepted."

Natasha's parents thought she was too young to marry. They insisted she wait a year.

"But I love him," she protested. "I really do. He's a dear, clever man."

"You must wait." They were immovable.

Andrew agreed. "It's only one year. Now I am recovered from my wounds, Natasha, I must rejoin the army to fight. The French are marching ever closer to Russia. We'll marry when I return. If, God forbid, trouble should come to you or your family, talk to Pierre. He has a heart of gold. He understands everything."

When Andrew departed, Natasha was utterly miserable. She went to live quietly in the country with her parents. But some months later, she received an invitation to stay with friends in Moscow and decided to accept.

In Moscow, she met Helene, Pierre's wife.

"You're too pretty a pearl to be buried in the country," Helene said. Helene had the gift of being able to flatter and sound natural. "You must visit me often. I have a mansion here in Moscow

as well as St. Petersburg, you know. I want you to meet my brother Anatole."

Anatole had run up vast debts in St. Petersburg, so his father, Prince Vasili, had sent him to sponge off Pierre in Moscow. Anatole had secretly married a Polish girl, but had abandoned her and was now pretending to be a bachelor. He believed in amusing himself whatever the consequences, never caring about the hurt he inflicted.

Natasha met Anatole at the opera. She could tell by the way he talked and laughed with her that he was enraptured by her. And, to her horror, something in her responded.

"Let me see you again," he begged. "Accept this flower as my pledge."

"Oh no," thought Natasha, "I am lost. What's happening to me?"

Fear overwhelmed her, because the barrier she thought was firmly between herself and other men had disappeared. Though she was engaged to Andrew, she felt bewitched by Anatole.

"Why not enjoy yourself?" laughed Helene, and because Helene was so much older, Natasha thought Helene must be right. There was no harm in simply going out with Anatole. No harm at all...

But Anatole had other intentions.

"I love you, sweet Natasha," he whispered. "Come away with me, be mine. I've already arranged a priest to marry us."

"I must love him or this wouldn't be happening," Natasha thought, believing everything Anatole said. She didn't know Anatole was already married; she had no idea the ceremony he'd organized was a mock wedding.

She wrote to Andrew, who was fighting far away, breaking their engagement, and to Helene, telling her everything. Helene informed Pierre that Natasha was about to run away with Anatole.

"WHAT?" Pierre thundered. "It's monstrous! Your brother is married already. What can he offer a young girl like Natasha except utter ruin! I must stop them immediately."

He raced to find Anatole. "You deceived Natasha. How dare you!" Pierre began, and saw him put on the same cringing smile that Helene wore when she wanted money. Disgusted, Pierre pulled out his wallet and withdrew a handful of notes. "Take all this. Now go away. Why don't you join the army and act like a real man?"

Next, he saw Natasha, still wrapped in her fur-lined cloak, awaiting the carriage Anatole had ordered for their elopement.

Pierre was furious at the way she'd treated Andrew. He couldn't understand how she could be so cruel.

Natasha grew deeply ashamed, unable to speak. Pity and tenderness welled up in Pierre as he realized how her feelings had carried her, powerless in a raging torrent, beyond reason, beyond safety.

"Did you love Anatole, that wicked man?"

"Don't call him wicked... Love him? Oh, I don't know..." She began to cry. "I still love Andrew, but he'll never forgive me."

"I fear you're right."

"All is over for me," she wept.

"Never that," Pierre comforted her. "I believe at heart you are good."

She wept now for gratitude. However badly she had behaved, she knew she had one true friend.

Chapter 7
The battle of Borodino

Onwards, relentless and unstoppable, the French army marched through eastern Europe... until they reached Russia.

Napoleon's aim was simple: France must rule the world. Europe should be one fatherland, Paris its capital, France the envy of all nations. Even if thousands died in his wars, his noble purpose, he felt, justified their deaths. This Russian war, he was convinced, made good sense. In the end, there would be prosperity for all.

Napoleon's new goal was to gain control of Moscow. On the way there, he led his army so magnificently that every skirmish on Russian soil was a victory for the French.

By the time the French got to Borodino, a village near Moscow, they numbered 133,000 soldiers, and the Russians only 120,000.

Borodino lay between flat fields of ripe corn, surrounded by small hills and forests. Here, Napoleon, certain of success, offered battle to the Russian generals, who accepted it.

Behind the hills and hidden in the forests, Napoleon stationed his men, planning their positions like a game of chess, ready for the attack. The flat ground, the battlefield, glittered bright silver with their bayonets.

Though the French were superior in strength and strategy, every Russian soldier's heart flamed with a yet more powerful weapon: real hatred of the enemy.

In Moscow, as news broke of the French drawing closer, fear was in the air. Families began to pack up their belongings and leave. The roads around Moscow were crowded with carriages, horses, carts, pedestrians. In the once bustling city, the streets began to echo eerily with emptiness. All were united in a desire to flee. Only a very few remained.

At Borodino, Andrew felt the battle would be the most terrible he'd ever fought. He gazed at a row of birch trees, their white branches and green leaves shining in the August sunshine, thinking, *If I die, all this will still exist... but not me...* He felt the scene change from beauty to something menacing, and a shiver ran down his spine.

He was surprised to recognize a man approaching him on horseback. "Pierre!" he cried. "What are you doing here? You're not in the army. You don't approve of war."

"I'm interested. I want to see what happens."

"Oh, we'll win. But war isn't a plaything for you, or for generals, or idle politicians wanting glory. We must be honest. It's horrible."

Wishing to cheer his friend, Pierre urged, "Natasha... she still loves you."

"Don't talk of her," Andrew snapped.

Several hundred French guns began firing.

Instantly, Andrew galloped off, yelling, "I'll never forgive her."

Pierre, astride his horse, saw, through the smoking mist of gunpowder, men charge and fall,

screaming. He heard cannonballs whistle and
strike with a deafening roar. As the booming
cannon fire grew more intense, so the field
of yellow corn grew thick and deep with
dead soldiers.

More than ever, Pierre hated war. Suddenly
dazzled by a flash of flame, he was thrown back...

When he came to, he saw the grass was
scorched, and his horse, like himself, was on the
ground, uttering prolonged and piercing cries.

But he was still alive.

Ten hours later, Napoleon was shaking his head
in disbelief. Despite everything being the same as

in his previous battles – preparation, organization, reinforcements brought in – this time there was no French victory. His invincible army was fleeing, unable to drive the Russians back. WHY? He could not understand it.

Andrew understood. He knew the Russians were winning the battle of Borodino because they drove themselves beyond their own expectations.

The result of a battle, as every soldier knows, is decided not by orders from on high, but by an invisible force called the spirit of the army.

On Andrew fought, amid the boom and thud of cannon. A shell dropped by him, and sent him tumbling to the ground. From his abdomen, blood poured out, staining the grass.

Is this death? I don't want to die... I love life, he thought, and knew no more as peasants lifted him off the battlefield.

He recovered consciousness in the field hospital, his wound bandaged and the torn flesh cut away. Next to him lay another wounded man, screaming as his leg was amputated, clotted with blood, the boot still on.

"Oh... oh..." sobbed the man.

Andrew saw it was Anatole. Still dazed, he could only just recall what Anatole had done to him. As memory flooded back fully, he thought of Natasha and how much he'd loved her. He realized he loved her still. Pity and forgiveness for both Natasha and Anatole filled his heart. He wept tender, loving tears for them, and, remembering the teachings of his childhood, *Love your enemies,* wept again for all the tens of thousands slain on the field of battle.

Chapter 8
The burning of Moscow

Napoleon felt as if he were in a nightmare. As the months moved into winter, the French army pushed on to reach their goal, Moscow, to find the Russians had retreated eighty miles beyond it.

The city itself was almost deserted. Worse,

it was burning. For weeks the sky glowed fiery red above blackened streets of charred buildings – ruined palaces, opera houses, shops, tenements, inns and bars.

Who can say how it happened? The French thought the Russians had burned their own city; the Russians blamed the French. The burning of Moscow was inevitable. It was built of wood. It was full of careless, starving, exhausted soldiers and a few angry inhabitants, all making camp fires, cooking, smoking, looting... and so it went up in flames.

The French had seized their prize to find, after all, it was worthless.

When Napoleon was told Moscow was empty, he paced to and fro. Instead of his expected entrance to the city as a conquering hero, he'd achieved nothing but an empty victory. The French army now resembled a hive of bees without their queen – lost, disordered, without direction. The soldiers fled from Moscow only to

face their next enemy: the cruel Russian winter.

It was too much for them. Frozen, lost, trying to get home and loathed by the Russians, one by one they died. The once glorious army was like an animal, suffering a slow death from its mortal blow received at Borodino. Napoleon's dream of world power was over.

Natasha was one of the last to leave Moscow. She was packing up her belongings in a carriage to

return to her parents, when she saw a convoy of wounded Russian soldiers.

"Can I help?" she called to the man in charge.

"Well, yes." The man pointed to a soldier who was barely conscious.

"You can take this one with you. He'll slow us down and he won't get better. You'd probably care for him better than we can."

It was Andrew. Two soldiers dragged him over to Natasha's carriage and lifted him in.

Natasha slipped a pillow under his head. His face looked so gentle, she was sure he was close to death.

He opened his eyes. "Natasha... How strange that fate has brought us together now."

Taking his hand, she touched it with her lips. "Forgive me."

"For what?"

"For what I have done," she faltered. "I love you more, better than before."

Seeing her eyes shining with love and compassion, he asked, with yearning, "Shall I live?"

"Oh, yes!" she cried out, stroking his hair.

"How good it would be..." he murmured, closing his eyes again.

Waking, he wondered, *What is love? Love is life. Love is everything. I understand everything because I love. To die means that I, a particle of love, shall return to its source.*

Summoning his last energy, he whispered, "My son, Nicholas... look after him..."

He didn't want to die, but death crept through the door of life and took him away.

Chapter 9
A heart of gold

When Pierre was at Borodino, he received a message about his wife. Helene had died suddenly in Moscow.

He rushed at once to Moscow and found it on fire. As he watched the tongues of flames under the rooftops with horror, a woman, a stranger, threw herself at his feet, screaming.

"My daughter! Don't let her burn!"

"Where is she?"

"In the house. We all escaped, but she..."

"I'll get her," Pierre promised.

He raced inside and found the child, who bit him like a terrified little animal as he snatched her up and carried her to safety.

After that, he stayed on in Moscow, helping wherever he could. His own house had escaped the fires.

As winter turned into spring, the three great events of the recent past: the death of Helene, the loss of Andrew and the terrible war, made him agonize: *What is life for?* The black gloom of doubt lifted at last when he found the answer: *Seek the good in everything. Grasp life and love it.*

He started to think about Natasha. How was she coping?

She was living in the country, he discovered, with her parents. When he visited her, she looked much older and careworn. They talked of Andrew.

"It was such happiness to see him... at the end," said Natasha, her voice breaking.

"He was calm? Not afraid of death? Yes, happiness indeed." Pierre leaned forward, his eyes full of tears.

It was a beginning. Love steals imperceptibly across time and circumstance into wounded hearts. Neither Pierre nor Natasha believed they were ready for new life and happiness, yet love awaited them.

She remembered Andrew's words: *Pierre has a heart of gold.*

He thought: *I cannot imagine life without her.*

They married. They lived truly happily ever after, surrounded by their children and Andrew's son, Nicholas.

"You're a wonderful father, Pierre," murmured Natasha, cuddling their newest baby.

Pierre put his arm around her with a contented sigh. He could still hardly believe how joyful his life had become.

And young Nicholas? He was an affectionate and intelligent little boy. He knew Pierre had been his father's friend, and guessed that his father had loved Natasha.

"I love Uncle Pierre," he told himself. "He's good and kind. But I will never forget my father. When I grow up, I will be brave like him. I will do something that would have made him proud."

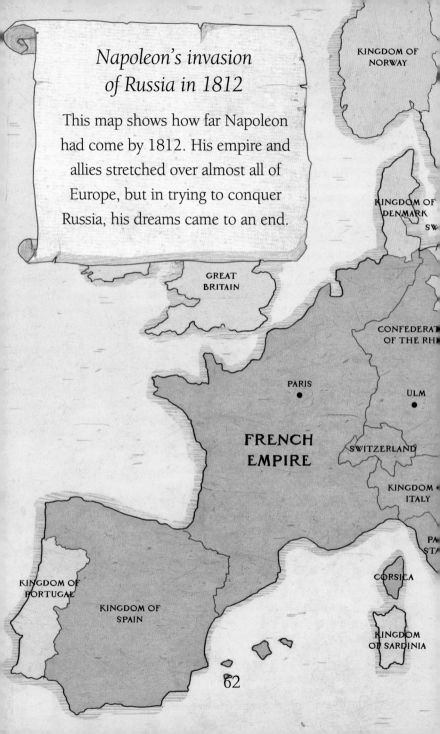

Napoleon's invasion of Russia in 1812

This map shows how far Napoleon had come by 1812. His empire and allies stretched over almost all of Europe, but in trying to conquer Russia, his dreams came to an end.

KINGDOM OF NORWAY

KINGDOM OF DENMARK

SW

GREAT BRITAIN

CONFEDERAT OF THE RH

PARIS

ULM

FRENCH EMPIRE

SWITZERLAND

KINGDOM ITALY

PA STA

CORSICA

KINGDOM OF PORTUGAL

KINGDOM OF SPAIN

KINGDOM OF SARDINIA

62

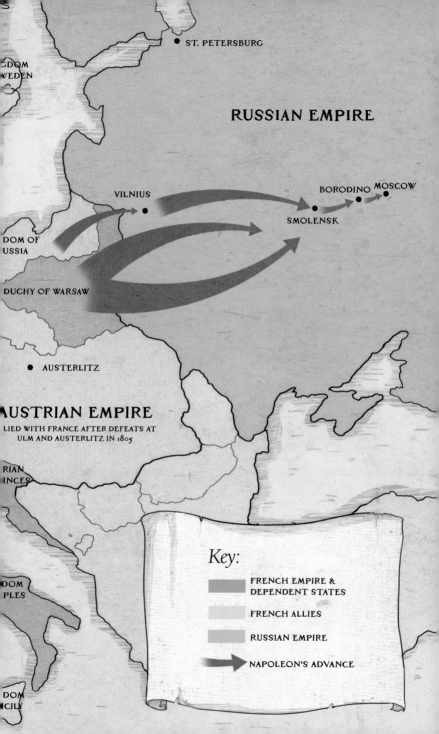

Leo (Lev Nikolayevich) Tolstoy 1828-1910

Leo Tolstoy was born in Russia on September 9th, 1828 to Count Nikolai Tolstoy and his wife. Both parents died when he was a boy and relatives brought him up.

After failing his university exams, he tried running the family estate. This wasn't wholly successful so, encouraged by his brother, he enlisted in the army. With time on his hands, he began to write. During the Crimean War, he wrote *Sevastopol Stories*. The tales were an instant success.

In 1862, he married Sofya Andreevna Behrs, and spent the next twenty years on his estate, bringing up his family, and writing. It was a time of huge turmoil in Russia. Tolstoy spent hours reflecting on life, philosophy, God and religion, all of which are discussed in *War and Peace* and *Anna Karenina*, the novel which followed.

Tolstoy died at the age of 82. Today, he is acclaimed as Russia's greatest novelist and *War and Peace* as one of the world's great novels. This adaptation gives a feel of the epic original, which has over a thousand pages filled with unforgettable characters, gripping situations and the grand sweep of history.